Thomas Ward

Flora, or the Gipsy's Frolic

SALZWASSER
VERLAG

Thomas Ward

Flora, or the Gipsy's Frolic

Reprint of the original, first published in 1858.

1st Edition 2023 | ISBN: 978-3-37515-234-5

Verlag (Publisher): Salzwasser Verlag GmbH, Zeilweg 44, 60439 Frankfurt, Deutschland
Vertretungsberechtigt (Authorized to represent): E. Roepke, Zeilweg 44, 60439 Frankfurt, Deutschland
Druck (Print): Books on Demand GmbH, In de Tarpen 42, 22848 Norderstedt, Deutschland

FLORA,

OR

THE GIPSY'S FROLIC;

A PASTORAL OPERA

IN THREE ACTS.

DRAMA AND MUSIC

BY

THOMAS WARD.

———————•———————

NEW YORK:

FRENCH & WHEAT, PRINTERS, No. 18 ANN STREET.

1858.

TO THE CENTURY:

AN ASSOCIATION ESTABLISHED FOR THE

PROMOTION OF HARMONY AND GOOD FEELING,

THIS WORK,

WRITTEN WITH A KINDRED PURPOSE,

IS RESPECTFULLY INSCRIBED
BY
A FELLOW-MEMBER.

PROLOGUE,

AS SPOKEN AT THE FIRST REPRESENTATION OF THE OPERA,

AT "LAND'S END," HUNTINGTON, L. I., JULY 30, 1857.

————◆————

THERE is a rapture that can never cloy—
A golden joy untarnished by alloy:
A present bliss unchased by coming sorrow,
That thrills to-day, yet leaves no pang to-morrow—
That wafts the soul to giddiest ecstasy
Without the sickening of a flight so high;
Charming, unsated—blooming without blight—
Returning still with ever new delight!
'Tis music!—what can boast so much of all
The poor delights that have survived the fall?
A joy so pure of stains, that will combine
With all of earth, must be indeed divine!
Yes! harmony first stirred our mortal ears
With the far hymnings of revolving spheres;
Music, with light, broke through the heavenly bars,
And song was taught us by the morning stars!

There are who doubtless deem it wondrous strange
The lyric drama, takes so wide a range:
Leaving great cities, where alone it throve,
To find a shelter in the field and grove—

Most strange of all—its roving steps should wend
To spot so lone as this extreme "Land's End."
Here where no minstrels broke the stilly flow,
Save whistling quail, or Ethiopian crow:
With cock sole tenor of the robust school,
Whose chorus were the croakers of the pool;
Whose treble notes the twittering swallow gave,
Whose bass the thunderous surgings of the wave.
No Mario here the damsel's hearts had tried,
Nor Grisi poured her oil upon the tide:
No squalls disturbed the rustic ear, save those
Which from cross babes, or rude nor'westers rose.
By these lone shores, and song-benighted ways,
We plant our mission, and our standard raise;
Nor deem our aim unprofitably wrong
To spread the culture of harmonious song:
And meet it seems her rovings here should close
'Mid the same scenes that cheered her when she rose.
For Song was born no sickly, city child,
But a free nymph that ranged the greenwood wild;
And, not until her simple youth had flown,
Luxurious grew, and sought the fevered town.
In Delphian groves first rang Apollo's lyre,
And hills Parnassian echoed first his choir:
On shores like these his conch old Triton blew,
And chanting syrens lured the hapless crew;
And shell of turtle, shrunk by solar fire,
Gave out the earliest hintings of the lyre.
So leading music to the shore and main,
We only bring her to her 'home again;
And render back unto the salt sea wave
Some portion of the harmony she gave;
And treat the groves to singing birds whose tone
Shall waken echoes rivalling their own.

In this bold venture in the realms of song,
It may be deemed by this judicial throng
Presumptuous, that a novice should aspire
To strike, with even a faltering hand, the lyre
Still quivering with the soul entrancing beat
Of gay Rossini, or Bellini sweet;
Or Donizetti, whose all-varied strain
Would seem to blend the graces of the twain;
Or Verdi brave—who, passing oft the true,
On anvils seeks to hammer something new;
Or him, the Raphael of the lyric art,
The tender, grand, immaculate Mozart!
Think not we seek with any boastful aim
To tilt with masters of the heights of fame:
For at their base are quiet nooks and springs,
Where humbler birds may plume their 'prentice wings;
Leaving the summit of the mountain hoar
To the bold pinions that have learned to soar.
These lowly paths, by guardian nature led,
With wary steps we venture now to tread;
Seeking to cull some wild flowers by the way—
With what success remains for you to say!
Whatever virtue in our strain may dwell
We promise this—it shall be rendered well;
For we have voices whose exulting range
Would soon our whistle to a trumpet change—
Yes! we have song-birds here within our cage
Shall move your souls to ecstasy or rage;
Warblers that vaulting in their bold career
The nightingale would hold his breath to hear;
Songsters, that prize their golden notes too high
For royal gifts, or Ullman's purse to buy,
Here meet, unpaid, to favor Art's good cause;
And ask no guerdon—save your fair applause!

DRAMATIS PERSONÆ.

LADY FLORA—*Daughter of the Lord of the Manor.*—CONTRALTO.

MARIE—*her Confidante.*

COUNT ERNEST.—*a Soldier, her Affianced Lover.*—BARITONE.

POPINJAY—*A Village Innkeeper.*—BASS.

DAME POPINJAY—*his Wife.*—MEZZO-SOPRANO.

JACQUES—*their Son.*

ANNETTE—*their daughter.*—SOPRANO.

CLAUDE—*a Peasant, her Lover.*—TENOR.

GIPSY GIRL.—MEZZO-SOPRANO.

PAUL—*a Servant of the Baron.*

CHORUS OF PEASANTS—*Men and Women.*

SCENE—France, on the borders of Switzerland.

DATE—The latter part of the reign of Louis XIV.

TIME OF ACTION—Two days.

ARGUMENT.

———————

POPINJAY, a village innkeeper, on the occasion of his daughter's birth-day, invites his friends and neighbors to a rustic fête; during which, Count Ernest, who is on his way to visit the Lady Flora after his return from the wars, stops awhile at the village to rest his horse; and is induced by the beauty of the queen of the fête, and the solicitations of the host to join the merry-making. The Gipsy girl is admitted to tell the fortunes, and promote the pleasure of the guests. She is a shrewd and mischievous, but not malicious creature; and soon per-ceives among the various ingredients of which the party is composed, much fitting material for the exercise of her wit, and love of frolic. She accordingly sets them severally by the ears, by working upon the vanity of Dame Popinjay to bore her husband for new finery—by ex-citing the coquetry of Annette to endeavor to attract the attention of the Count, to the great discomfiture of Claude, her rustic lover—and, lastly, by drawing the attention of the highly sensitive Lady Flora to this seeming infidelity of her lover, while rambling *tête-a-tête* with the village queen—all this necessarily produces a state of general *em-brouillement*, which terminates the first act.

In the second act the men are discovered seeking consolation in wine for the estrangement of their several mates; and the Gipsy, having had her frolic, begins to feel some remorse at the extent to which the contending parties have carried their controversies; and resolves to re-concile those whom so lately she had playfully sought to divide. She

induces Claude, the village minstrel, to soften his coquettish mistress
with a serenade, and warns her of the danger of driving her lover to
the wars by her unkindness. She persuades Dame Popinjay that she
will more surely succeed in her wishes with her husband by ceasing to
annoy him with her importunities; and finally, in the third act, bribes
the farrier to lame the Lady Flora's horse, so that she is obliged to
leave the chase, and dismount at the village in the neighborhood of the
Count; where she solemnly warns her that her lover, though guilty of
a little pardonable gallantry, is not unfaithful to her; and shrewdly
recommends that his fidelity be tested by exposing him once more to
the fascinations of the village belle, who is privy to the scheme. Marie,
the *confidante*, urges the justice of this course; and the Lady, after a
highly exciting struggle with her pride, finally consents to the plot;
which results in the complete vindication of the Count, and his recon-
cilation with the Lady. Their happiness soon contagiously affects the
rustic lovers; and brings on a state of general good feeling, to the
great satisfaction of the Gipsy; who is discovered, in the end, to be
one of Popinjay's children, who was stolen away in her infancy by a
band of roving Gipsies that chanced to pass that way.

FLORA;

OR,

THE GIPSY'S FROLIC.

———◆———

ACT I.

SCENE I.—*A Village Green at sunrise, with prepara-
tions for a fête. A Cottage Inn on one side.*

CHORUS—*Without.*

PEASANTS. What ho ! pretty maids—good morn !
PEASANT GIRLS. Good morn ! good friends—a merry good morn !
PEASANTS. Then hey for the fête ! Come all ! ·
PEASANT GIRLS. We come !   [*They enter.*

ALL. We come ! we come ! from lake and field,
And bring the spoil the meadows yield ;
For here are fruits, and here are flowers,
To grace our gay and festive hours.

PEASANTS. The skies are all bright with a glorious day !
PEASANT GIRLS. And our hearts are as full of the sunshine as they !

ALL.
> We come from the lake,
> We come from the field,
> And bring the spoil
> The meadows yield :
> We come with our fruits,
> We come with our flowers,
> To grace the gay and festive hours.
> Then sing of the joys
> Of the bold sailor boys !
> Come sing !

TRIO—*Barcarole.*

O'er the waters bright and clear,
Heaving, glancing, merrily dancing—
What care we for billows prancing ?
We can ride them without fear !
O ! what joy—O ! what joy—as we bound along,
When the rosy west is glowing—
When the moon her face is showing—
Wafted by the breath of song

ALL
> We come from the lake,
> We come from the field,
> And bring the spoil
> The meadows yield :
> We come with our fruits,
> We come with our flowers,
> To grace the gay and festive hours.
> Then sing of the joys
> Of the brave mountain boys !
> Come sing !

TRIO—*Mountaineers' Song.*

Up the steep with Alpine spear
Leaping, racing, chamois chasing
What care we when glaciers facing ?
We can follow without fear !
O ! what joy—O ! what joy—as we bound along
When peaks are red with morning shining,
Or valleys weep at days declining,
Buoyant with the breath of song.

CHORUS.—Up the steep, &c.

Enter POPINJAY *and* DAME POPINJAY *from the house.*

POP. Welcome! welcome friends, and neighbors all!
(*shaking hands,*) we're heartily glad to see you. With such
a goodly company I'm sure we'll have a good time of it.
We've met together on this occasion, to keep our daughter
Annette's birthday, and make ourselves as merry as we
can. You know I like to see everybody happy about me.
But wife, I say, where is the girl? she should be the first
to welcome her friends. But the jade was always a heed-
less . child, and although she has eighteen years on her
head, I fear has not yet reached the age of discretion.

DAME P. Come, come, Mr. Popinjay, I won't hear you
run down our little pet in that way.

POP. I don't mean to run her down, my dear, I'm sure—
the baggage is not a bad child, as times go—only . a little
giddy now and then, as girls will be.

JACQUES. Ah! yes, dad, she *is* a bad child—a prodi-
giously unprofitable progeny; I'm the only real comfort the
old folks have.

POP. You! you young rascal! yes, you are a great
comfort to your parents indeed. Why friends! that chap
fairly worries the life out of me. He's at some mischief or
other from morning till night.

JACQUES. What? I sir, consider dad, what you're ejacu-
lating, and before company too!

POP. Yes, you, sirrah! with your long face. In
short, we've tried our best to make something out of him,
and the good Baron sent him to school for a couple of
years, but all he picked up, that I can see, was a few big
words, which I'm sure the young rogue does not know the
meaning of himself. He's always in mischief, and so tor-
ments the neighbors that they've dubbed him "Bother-
ation." The lad is reckless to boot, and once badly
wounded his little sister with an arrow. Why, only last

Michælmas, when the good Curé dined with us, and Mrs. P. had prepared some of her famous whipped syllabub for dessert, that young scapegrace ate it all up secretly, and then put soap-suds in its place; and the Curé's wry face when he tasted it, and Mrs. P.'s look of blank horror were a sight to behold! Oh! he's a precious comfort to his parents indeed! *[All laugh.*

DAME P. Come now Mr. P., don't be too hard upon the poor boy. He's only full of youthful spirits.

POP. Youthful spirits indeed!

Enter CLAUDE, *with a guitar.*

POP. Ah! here comes Master Claude. Welcome neighbor! (*shakes hands,*) right welcome! Now friends, our fête shall not flag for lack of a song; for this gallant is the daintiest minstrel in the whole country round.

CLAUDE. [*Bowing.*] A merry meeting to you all! But where is Annette? I don't find her among you.

POP. No doubt you're anxious to see her, friend Claude. We all know your liking for the girl, though she does lead you a dance, they say. But, never mind that—stick to her boy! you're a good lad, and I like you—stick to her, bravely, I say—she must give in at last—women never can be long of one mind.

DAME P. There! there you go, Mr. P., always railing at our sex.

POP. Well, well, wife! I'll say no more against women. We won't quarrel about *such* trifles on Annette's birthday.

CLAUDE. But what keeps her? What can she be doing?

POP. Doing? why prinking, I suppose, just what the girls are always doing.

DAME P. Well, really Mr. P., I must say——

CLAUDE. Ah! here she comes! here she comes!

Enter ANNETTE, *singing, from the house.*

ALL. Long live Annette! long live Annette!

ANN. Thanks! thanks, my kind friends—many thanks!
You are all too good, I'm sure.   [*Shaking hands.*

CLAUDE. How beautiful she looks!   [*Aside.*

ANN. Father, your blessing!

POP. There—bless you, my child!

P. GIRL. Look, Annette! see what we have brought
you for your birthday!   [*Offering flowers &c.*

ANN. Oh! what pretty things! and all for me?

CHORUS, *with soprano solo, of peasant girls making presents. They crown*
ANNETTE *with flowers.*

Let these sweetly breathing flowers
On thy brow and breast be laid;
There, as in their native bowers,
Will they feel at home, sweet maid!

ANNETTE.

Thanks, I will wear these fair gifts of the day
On my brow and my breast, till they're faded away;
And still, when their glory is withered and fled,
Will I prize them the more for the sweets they have shed.
CHORUS.—Let these sweetly breathing flowers, &c.

CLAUDE. Come, Annette, you have not said a single
word to me, to-day. Won't you shake hands?

ANN. Nonsense! *No,* I tell you.

CLAUDE. What! not on your birthday?

ANN. Well, if I must, there! [*Offers her hand, and as
he goes to take it, jerks it away coquettishly, and runs off.*

Enter PAUL.

POP. Silence friends! a messenger from the Baron!

PAUL. My master, the baron sends his warm congratula-
tions to all present on this joyful occasion; and regrets
that an attack of his old enemy, the gout, will prevent his
joining your merry party to-day; but is happy in being
able to send a fair representative in the person of the Lady

Flora, who will shortly grace the meeting with her presence. Meanwhile he proffers a token of his regard for Mademoiselle Annette in this box, and for Mr. Popinjay in this sealed package. [*Exit.*

DAME P. A sealed package! Oh! how I should like to know what is in it!

POP. I dare say you would. Come, stand aside all! give us room. [*Opens the package.*] A parchment, I declare!

DAME P. A parchment! what can it be? I wonder if it's a diploma?

POP. And why not wife? There's many a greater blockhead than your old hubby has been made an L.L.D. before to-day.

ALL. Read it! Read it!

POP. [*Putting on his specs.*] Well—let's see—let s see: "To all to whom these presents may come, greeting. This Indenture witnesseth that out of the great regard in which I hold my old and faithful tenant, Peter Popinjay—[*While P. is reading* JACQUES *puts his head between him and the parchment. P. cuffs him.*]—I do hereby grant and convey to him, his heirs and assigns forever, all that certain inn, and plot of ground on which he resides, commonly known as 'The Briar Cottage,' with all the lands, tenements, and heriditer-ari-ments, &c." Why, wife! the good Baron has given us the Briar Cottage!

DAME P. Oh, Peter! what a lucky day! The Briar Cottage ours! with all the heriditer-ari-ments——

ALL. Long life to the Baron!

POP. This is great news indeed! why, wife, [*strutting about together,*] we are landed proprietors! stand aside, good friends—[*with mock dignity*]—stand aside, all! and make way for the landed proprietors! But don't be alarmed! we are not going to be proud, friends! your children may still play with ours upon the same green together!

DAME P. But, Mr. P., we must, of course, adopt a different style of dress and living. I must certainly have a wardrobe suitable to our elevated condition.

Pop. Nonsense, wife, I tell you seriously you'll find no change in me, and if our good luck is going to turn your head, why, I would rather our kind landlord would e'en take his favors back again.

Enter a Peasant Girl.

Peasant Girl. O! look girls, look! here's a stranger gentleman, just dismounted from his horse, and coming this way. He has gold lace all over his coat, and a gold sword by his side. Oh! he's the beautifullest man!

Pop. A stranger! who can it be?

Enter Count Ernest.

Count. Pardon my intrusion, my good friends! I am a traveler, a friend of your landlord, the Baron. I have stopped a while at your village to rest my horse, who is somewhat fagged after a hard morning's gallop.

Pop. Oh! there's no intrusion, your Excellence! this is our daughter's birthday, sir, and we should feel proud if any friend of the good Baron would honor our merry-making with his company.

Dame P. Certainly, sir. Oh, do stay, sir! this is our cottage, sir, with all the heriditer-ari-ments—we are landed proprietors, sir!

Pop. [*Aside to* Dame P.] Hold your foolish tongue!

Count. Your daughter's birthday, is it? and pray which is the queen of the fête?

Ann. I am father's daughter, sir. [*Courtseying.*

Count. [*Aside.*] What sweet simplicity! A charming rural queen to be sure—well, my kind friends, since you will have it so, I'll join your festivities. My horse will be all the better for a few hours' rest.

Pop. You are heartily welcome, sir!

COUNT. Thanks! thanks! [*To* ANNETTE.] And now my pretty little rose-bud, how happens it that you have not yet been chosen to adorn the home of some honest lad? You must surely have a lover?

ANN. [*Looking askance at* CLAUDE.] A sort of one, sir.

COUNT. Ah! a sort of lover? But one not altogether satisfactory, I suppose; and yet he seems to be a worthy, good lad, too. [CLAUDE *bows.*] Well, come now, my little beauty, tell me frankly what kind of a lover you would like!

Song.—ANNETTE.

I long for a lover, choice and rare,
  But where to find him is the task,
For whether he's tall or dark or fair
  Is not the question I should ask!
  Is it a question I should ask?
No, no, I seek for a lover whose flame
Burns through all trial still true and the same,
Through sunshine and tempest, in grief and in glee,
Oh! such is the lover—the lover for me!

And could I win a lofty prize,
  My dainty heart would dare refuse;
For that he is rich, or great, or wise,
  Is not the reason I would choose.
Is it a reason I should choose?
      No, no, I seek, &c.,

Methinks I hear it gravely said,
  So dainty a heart its chance may lose—
Well! better far to die a maid,
  Than in hot haste to rashly choose.
  Should I for this unwisely choose?
, No! still I'll hope for a lover whose flame, &c.

COUNT. A charming description of a lover indeed! and of the right stamp; but I cannot help thinking, my pretty maid, unless appearances are strangely deceitful, that you need not seek far to find the very kind of lover you describe so glowingly. [*Looking at* CLAUDE, *who bows.* *To* CLAUDE.] Come hither, my lad—you have a figure for a soldier. Egad! I should like to enlist you into my regiment. How would you like a soldier's life?

CLAUDE. I'm sure I should like it, sir, mightily.

ANN. Don't think of it, Claude! It must be a hard life.

COUNT. A soldier's life a hard one? not a whit. A little rough at times, to be sure, but the very life for a stout youngster like this. And then, he'd become the pride of the village—honored by the men, and adored by the women!

Song.—COUNT ERNEST.

Oh! give me the life of the gallant soldier!
  Roving, careless, gay and free;
Roam where he will, he is welcome ever,
  Pet of the fair ones all is he.
Then he'll march, he'll march when duty calls him,
  To front the bloody field:
His country's prop, no foe appals him
  In danger's hour to yield.
When the loud drum beats, 'mid the clang of arms,
What fire his bosom warms!
  Soon o'er the din of battle,
  And the dreadful cannon's rattle,
  The trumpet sounds to victory!
  And far and wide the joyful echoes fly!
Then gaily will he bound, all his trials overcome,
With his laurel honors crowned, and a welcome home.
Oh! give me the life of the gallant soldier!
  Happy still in every state,
In life wreathed by beauty, and in death crowned by glory,
  Oh! give me the gallant soldier's fate!

POP. Why, you make me feel like shouldering a musket myself, sir! Ah, well, I have seen the day when I could march with the best of them, but that was years ago, before

I was hampered with a wife, and so many other incumbrances.

COUNT. This, then, is not your only child?

POP. Oh! bless you, no, sir! Providence has been quite bountiful to us in that particular. Would you like to see the list?   [*Pulling out a roll of paper.*

COUNT. What! do you keep a list of your children?

POP. And why not, sir? For, you see, as a man gets along in life, his memory will fail him sometimes, and I find it convenient to keep a written list always ready for occasion; so that whether I'm dealing out barley sugar for the good ones, or birch rods for the naughty, each one is sure to get his due share of what is going round, whether it be sweet or bitter. Here they are! all in a string! A good baker's dozen of them, sir, barring the little girl that was lost—aye! and a pair of twins at the end of the list, too!

COUNT. Well, upon my word, my worthy friend, Providence has smiled upon you indeed! I could not have supposed your family to be so numerous, for your good dame looks more like a daughter than a wife.

DAME P. [*Courtseying.*] Oh, sir! you are too polite, really.

JACQUES. Why, la! sir, a redundancy of children is not a matter of any sort of complexity. Now, there's Mrs. Soapsuds the washerwoman—why, she has seventeen, sir! All sizes, and no ablutionary assistance neither.

COUNT. Seventeen! amazing! and how does she manage, my little man, to take care of them all, and to carry on her business at the same time.

JACQUES. Simplest thing in the world, sir. As fast as she hangs out a piece of linen habiliment to dry, she puts a child astride the line for a clothes pin!   [*All laugh.*

POP. Ha! ha! ha! He has a knack at a story, that boy, and no wonder, for at school he was rated the best speaker and player of them all. They used to put the Old Testament stories on the stage, and what part do you think

he played, sir? Why, Sampson! That cock-sparrow—
that whippersnapper, must play the mighty Sampson!
Ha! ha!

JACQUES. I never told you, dad, why I was so fond of
enacting that muscular Biblical representative.

POP. Never; well, out with it, wiseacre!

JACQUES. Simply, because nobody can play the part of
Sampson without bringing down the house!

POP. Ha, ha, ha! Do you take, sir? Bringing down
the house! [Clapping his hands.

COUNT. Not so bad. He's a veritable chip of the old
block, to be sure.

ANN. Father! here's the Gipsy girl outside, she wants to
join the fête.

POP. Don't ask me, my girl! you know I never could
bear the sight of that vagrant race, since they stole away
our little child.

COUNT. What! had you indeed a child stolen by gipsies?

POP. Alas, yes, sir! It must have been some dozen
years ago or more, come Whitsuntide, when it happened.
She was a bright little black-eyed darling, and a great pet
among us all, and was last seen in the grove yonder, play-
ing with the gipsies; who drew the mother aside to tell
her fortune, and then enticed the child beyond her reach
All search was made, but she was never heard of more.

ANN. But, father, this Gipsy-girl could have had no
hand in that matter. She must have been too young at
the time. Oh, do let her in! we want her to tell us our
fortunes. She will make so much sport.

PEASANT GIRLS. Oh, yes, good Mr. Popinjay! do let her in!

POP. Well, well, girls, I won't baulk your humor. You
know, I can refuse you nothing, you little baggages, when
you come coaxing around me in this way; besides, I suppose we should forbid nobody on a day like this.

[They beckon to GIPSY, who enters with tambourine.

Song.—GIPSY.

Down the greenwood valleys I roam,
Sure 'neath heaven to find a home,
Under the hedgerow, or under the tree—
What does it matter? 'Tis all one to me!
　　'Tis all one to me!

Then when the tempest is clanging about,
Let it rage as it will—for my heart it is stout;
Come thunder, come sunshine, so that I be free—
What does it matter? 'Tis all one to me!
　　'Tis all one to me!

Maidens! I'll show you the face of your mate,
And lads! I will tell you the secrets of fate:
Or wretched, or happy, whatever it be—
What does it matter? 'Tis all one to me!
　　'Tis all one to me!

[*The crowd gather around* GIPSY, *holding out their hands.*

ANN. Come, here's money! tell us our fortunes!
　　　　　[GIPSY *looks at* ANNETTE'S *hand.*
GIPSY.　Wayward, giddy, coy coquette,
　　　Beware! thou shalt be conquered yet!
　　　　　　　[*Examines the* COUNT'S *hand.*
Sorrow first, at friends estranged,
Soon to rapture to be changed;
Sorrow, that the spirit bends—
Rapture, that will make amends.
　　　　　[*Then looks at* POPINJAY'S *hand.*
A tempest overhead shall break,
That even the aged oak will shake—　[P. *starts.*
Yet faint not! soon the storm goes past,
And all is sunshine at the last!
POP. I'll believe as much of that as I please, Miss Gipsy.
Your dark warnings shall not stop our frolic to-day, I can

tell you. Come, young folks, I wan't to stir you all up a little. Clear the ground for a dance. Won't your honor choose a partner?

COUNT. That I will, right gladly! I'll take a turn with our little queen here.

POP. Come, old lady! you must be lively, to-day!

[*Dances with* DAME P.

[*A dance. After the dance, all move up and down the stage. The* GIPSY *comes forward.*

GIPSY. [*Aside.*] And now, before the day is old,
    To raise the tempest I've foretold,
    All without aid of sorcery,
    Save such as human hearts supply:
    I know their secret caves, where sleep
    The passion-winds that rouse the deep.
                [*Leading the* COUNT *forward.*
    Regard the queen! and there espy
    A jewel worth a soldier's eye.

COUNT. It needs no magic, you little witch, to make that discovery; the village belle is beautiful, indeed, and I shall doubtless be well amused during my brief halt, in sharing the sports of this rustic fête.

[*The* COUNT *passes on.* GIPSY *leads forward* ANNETTE.

GIPSY.   Should beauty mate with clowns, that might
    Find favor with a gallant knight?

ANN. Nonsense! you try to flatter me. [*Aside.*] And yet my gentleman does keep his eye upon me a great deal. I'll humor him a little.

[ANNETTE *moves on.* GIPSY *stops* DAME P., *who is passing.*

GIPSY. [*Admiringly.*] A form so fine might put to shame
    The pride of many a noble dame—

Pity it were not robed in guise
More fit to meet admiring eyes !

DAME P. [*Aside.*] Come now, that's a very civil speech
for a Gipsy, and there's truth in it too—it *is* a great pity
that my wardrobe is so scanty, that I have never been able
to do justice to my figure, or to appear to any advantage
before company. But I'm resolved to bear it no longer.
Old Pop shall loosen his purse-strings, or I'll worry his life
out.

POP. Now, lads ! lend a hand here, and let's carry our
provender under the trees yonder. We'll spread the cloth
there presently. Come, form a line now, and march in
order like a band of gallant volunteers !

Pic-Nic March and Chorus.

Chorus.   Forward ! forward to the field !
                   Every danger we defy !
                   Not a man of our host shall yield,
                   That assaults the venison pie !

POP.   Should the tempest fire his guns
          At our gallant band as we dine,
       Boldly standing underneath, we'd defy him to the teeth,
          While we shed the precious blood of the vine !
                   Chorus. Forward ! forward &c.,

CLAUDE.
       When the fray is done, and the day is won,
          How cheerly homeward, we'll be returning !
       Having nothing killed but time, wounding hearts our only crime,
          And love's flames the only fires left burning !
                   Chorus. Forward ! forward, &c.

ALL.   Then hail ! hail to the glorious strife !
          Whose weapons are only the fork and the knife ;
       And that leaveth no widows, nor orphans to sigh,
          Save such as are found in the stall or the sty !

[*All march about the stage, and then move off. The* COUNT *with* ANNETTE. CLAUDE *remains.*

CLAUDE. I don't quite like Annette's flirting so much with that soldier gentleman. She is always too fond of strangers. But what does it matter to me? 'Tis plain she cares nothing for me, and I am a fool to be hanging about her in this way. I have a great mind to leave her, and go for a soldier. O, that I could learn whether I shall ever be able to win her! I'll seek the Gipsy—she might read my fate in the stars.

Song.—CLAUDE.

Tell! O tell me!
Tell, ye stars above me!
Will she learn to love me?
Alas! how weary—to see, to hear thee—
　Unloved though loving, and charmed though pining:
Yet such my folly, I linger near thee,
　To watch the glory, on others shining.
Thy voice may chide me, thy glance may chill,
And yet 'tis beauty—'tis music still!
　Oh dreary lot! Oh cruel fate!
　Why longer bear this hopeless state?
I'll to the wars with a gallant grace!
　Seeking at least a nobler life;
Better the soldier's storms to face
　Than waste in this unworthy strife!
Glory alone my soul shall move,
And Honor mount the throne of Love.
　To the wars! to the wars!
Oh cruel wars, that bid me leave her!
　But can I leave her?
　　Ah, no! ah, no!
　Tell! Oh tell me!
　Tell, ye stars above me!
　Will she learn to love me? 　　　　[*Exit.*

Enter Mr. *and* Mrs. Popinjay, *quarelling.*

Pop. Shame on you, Mrs. P.! to be annoying our friends by your folly. I tell you I have not the means to purchase this finery for you; and if I had, it would only be ridiculous in you to wear it.

Dame P. Come now, Mr. P., don't let us fall out on a day like this.

Pop. Well, well, wife; I'm not disposed to have hard words with you, I'm sure; only, don't make a fool of yourself before folks.

Dame P. That's right, honey, be kind. Now he's her own lovey-dovey again—he is.   [*Wheedling.*

Pop. Ah! darling, there's no resisting you, when you are in a good humor.

Comic Duet.—Popinjay *and* Dame Popinjay.

Dame P.	Dear Mr Popinjay !
Pop.	Well, duck, what would you say ?
Dame P.	Why, I was thinking what a very kind, obliging man you are !
Pop.	Nay, Mrs. Popinjay !
Dame P.	Well, love, what would you say ?
Pop.	Indeed you flatter me—'tis you that are the kindest creature far.
Both.	Look round the world—where can we see Twin hearts so happy as we ! [*Lovingly.*

Dame P.	Ah, dearest Popinjay !
Pop.	Well, darling, prate away !
Dame P.	When you would treat your pet, I've found a bonnet that will make you stare.
Pop.	Hem ! Mrs. Popinjay !
Dame P.	Ah! I know what you'll say.
Pop.	For such extravagance, Madame, I've not a dollar now to spare.
Both.	In all my life I never knew { A man so stingy as you. A wife so reckless as you. } [*Angrily.*

DAME P.   You horrid Popinjay,
              I don't care what you say !
              You paltry Popinjay,
              I'll pay you off some day !
              You surly Popinjay, you wretched Popinjay,
              You ugly Popinjay !

POP.   What a clatter ! what's the matter ?
              Why, Mrs. Popinjay ! why, Mrs. Popinjay !

BOTH.   Look round the world—where can we see ⎱ *Dolefully*.
              Two fools so wretched as we ? ⎰

                                       [Exeunt, different ways.

Enter COUNT, *following* ANNETTE.

COUNT. Why leave me so soon, pretty one ? I have not yet made you a birthday present ; so take this ring, and keep it in remembrance of the stranger whom the chances of life once enabled, for a brief hour, to be happy with you.

ANN. Oh, sir, that is too handsome for poor Annette.

                                         [Taking it.

COUNT. Come now ! and let us wander through the grove. The air is sweet, the birds are singing joyously, and all nature seems to invite us. Come !   *[Exeunt.*

As they move off, enter LADY FLORA, MARIE, GIPSY, *and* PAUL.

GIPSY. The lady fain the queen would see,
           Behold her in good company ! *[Exit, pointing.*

FLORA. [*With astonishment.*] Can I trust my eyes ? 'Tis Ernest ! and evidently seeking to win the love of that peasant girl. The long-waited-for come at last—but better gone—forever gone! than come so unworthily ! Oh, Ernest !

                                        [With feeling.

MARIE. Don't take it so deeply to heart, my lady. He cannot be making love to Annette.

FLORA. Not making love ? What, then, is love-making ?

Is secretly walking together, smiling together, whispering together, love-making ?—if not, I know not what are the evidences of passion. . Look, Marie ! mark how he draws her arm in his ! see ! how they bend their heads together ! [*Turning away.*] Oh, heavens ! and this is the man to whom for twelve long months I have devoted every thought—every feeling of my heart—dreaming only of him —longing only for his return ! Oh, Marie ! I am sick— sick of the world, and all around 'me ! [*Much affected.*

MARIE. Oh, my lady, it grieves me much to see you so distressed.

FLORA. [*Recovering herself.*] I am foolish to give way to this weakness. I came hither to. congratulate Annette on her birthday, and to present her with this chain ; but I have now no heart for this fête. Here, good Marie ; take you the chain to Annette in my name—I could not meet her now. Go, I will await you here. [*Exit* MARIE.] Oh, Ernest, Ernest ! and is this the return you make for all my constancy—my absolute devotion of every faculty to your dear memory during our long separation ? Oh ! are the happy hours. we spent so joyously together now no longer remembered ? Is there no twilight lingering from their golden glow ? Oh, treacherous, happy hours ! that were so brief, and yet so sweet in passing.

Song.—FLORA.

Trust not the happy hours !
That win our love, then cast away ;
    Far travelers from a land sublime,
    And strangers to our rugged clime,
They smile, and make no stay.
    Trust not the happy hours !

Oh, gems of dew—not stone !
That cheat the flowers of. youthful morn,

With winged stars, that light and fly,
Impatient for their native sky,
And leave the heart forlorn.
Trust not the happy hours !

Ah ! cruel, happy hours !
Ye wild birds of remorseless spring !
Why blind us with your golden coats ?
Why madden us with your ravishing notes ?
Forsaking as ye sing—
Trust not the happy hours !

Trust not the happy hours !
Yet who that feels could fail to trust ?
Alas ! to shun the crowning bliss
Of even a passing angel's kiss
Is not in mortal dust.
Trust not the happy hours !

FLORA. After what I have seen, I am resolved to hold
no interview with him—to have no explanation—but to
send him my decision by letter, and to part with him at once
and forever !

Enter COUNT ERNEST.

COUNT. [*With ardor.*] Flora, dearest Flora ! do we
meet at last ? [*She repulses him.*] Why this cruel coldness ? Flora ! speak ! Can it be possible that you have
outgrown the affection you once bore me ? This, then,
accounts for your long silence, which I fondly attributed
to the miscarriage of your letters.

FLORA. [*Haughtily.*] Spare your eloquence, Sir Count !
'Tis well contrived to cast reproach of fickleness upon me
in advance of the just retribution for your own falsehood,
which you so thoroughly deserve !

COUNT. I false ! Flora, believe it not. Either your
impetuous nature has hurried you into error ; or else some
enemy has abused your too credulous ear.

FLORA. It is not what I have heard, but what I have *seen*, Count Ernest, which convinces me that I have thrown away my affections upon one unstable as water.

COUNT. Haughty girl! some fit of wounded pride disturbs you.

FLORA. Call it pride, or what you will—it is at least a feeling that obliges me to vindicate the dignity of my sex, by instantly releasing you from all engagements contracted with me, and promptly terminating all intercourse between us.

COUNT. But hear me! Cruel girl! will you judge me without a hearing?

FLORA. There needs no hearing—no sophistry could avail against the evidence of the senses. But why prolong this humiliating interview, when these very eyes have been the fatal witnesses of your unworthiness? Enough! my resolution is taken—we part from this moment. Farewell.

COUNT. But—Flora——

FLORA. No more—it is too late!

Duet.—COUNT and FLORA.

FLORA.	Farewell!
COUNT.	Say not Farewell!
BOTH.	Alas the happy hours, Are gone like passing flowers!
FLORA.	And we must part!
COUNT.	No, no—I cannot part with thee! Ah! cruel maid—forgive me!
FLORA.	No! no! thou didst deceive me! Farewell! the die is cast.
COUNT.	Ah! fly me not! I'll love thee ever—
FLORA.	I cannot trust thee. Hence deceiver—
COUNT.	Yes! I will love thee ever! I will leave thee never Ah, hear me speak—my heart will break!
FLORA.	No! I can trust thee nevermore.
COUNT.	Ah, leave me not, dear maid!

FLORA. The parting hour is come!
Alas! the golden hours?
BOTH. How sweetly did they glide along!
With all the joys of youth and song!
FLORA. Ne'er to return.
COUNT. Yet' they may return;
Still let me see thee! still let me hear thee!
I'll ne'er deceive thee. O do not fear me!
FLORA. Farewell, deceiver! farewell forever!
Inconstant, go! farewell—farewell!

Enter all the characters.

POP. And so this is the lady's lover that she has been expecting so long!

ANN. Yes—and to quarrel at their first meeting—what a pity!

POP. A great pity, indeed! and what with the quarrel between you and Claude, and that of the Count and the lady——

JACQUES. Don't forget, dad, the tiff between yourself and my maternal ancestor!

POP. Out on you, scape-grace! what with all these disagreements, I say, our merry-making is likely to find a sad conclusion—and that meddling Gipsy's prophecy will come to pass after all.

GIPSY comes forward.

GIPSY.—*Recitative.*

The storm blows cold,
That I foretold
To wake the village wonder;
Now will I ride
Upon the tide,
And revel in the thunder!

FLORA; OR,

FINALE.—*Sestet and Chorus.*

Alas! how oft the fair young day,
Goes forth in smiles upon his way;
Nor dreams 'mid skies of blue, how soon
The storm may burst upon his noon:
The thunder rolls his drum profound,
The din of discord rings around,
And o'er the heavens that glowed with bloom
Is hung the appalling tempest gloom.
Ah! thus our day that rose so bright
Is setting in a cloudy night!
And hearts that blossomed with the morn
Are now by stormy passions torn!

END OF ACT I.

ACT II.

AFTERNOON OF THE SAME DAY.

SCENE I.—*The village green as before.*

COUNT, POPINJAY, CLAUDE, JACQUES, *and others, seated at a table under the trees, drinking.*

CHORUS.

> When the burning sky,
> Drains all nature dry,
> And when clouds let 'fly,
>   Their thunder!
> When we melt, and stew,
> Dripping through and through, (whew.)
> Oh! what can we do,
>   I wonder?

Pop.	I've a dose will cure—	
Chorus.	Don't deceive us!	
Pop.	'Twill relieve, I'm sure—	
Chorus.	Then relieve us.	
Pop.	Behold! 'tis wine!	[*Showing a bottle.*
Chorus.	Wine! ha! ha!	
Pop.	Is't not a noble cure?	
All.	When the burning sky, &c.,	

When the tempests blow,
Driving as they go,
Covering wide with snow,
   All under—
When we shake and freeze,
When we cough and sneeze,   [*Coughing*.
What will give us ease
   I wonder!

POP.   I've a dose will cure, &c.

COUNT. Ha! ha! ha! not so bad, by Bacchus! [*To* CLAUDE.] And now, my young troubadour!—my cornet that is to be—fill a bumper!—and sing us something in praise of the immortal fruit of the vine!

CLAUDE. I fear I could not please your excellence! My head is weak for drinking, and I have no vein for that kind of song.

COUNT. O ho! my fine youngster—you like not wine for fear of the head-ache, eh! yet you can sing love songs by the yard in praise of women, who will give you a pang an hundred fold sharper—the heart-ache!

JACQUES. My sentiments to a decimal fraction! A pair of bright eyes would always inflame my sensorium more than a dozen cups of wine.

POP. Bah! baby. What do you know about it?

COUNT. Listen, and I will prove my words.

Song.—COUNT.

Oh, weak and fool-hardy young lover,
   To substitute woman for wine!
The glow of whose charms, you'll discover,
   Fires more than the juice of the vine.

Who barters for beauty his whiskey,
   The change will be certain to rue;
For her eyes shed a spirit more frisky
   Than lurks in the best "mountain-dew."

Ah! those eyes, at each meeting so merry,
    You'll find to outsparkle champagne;
And ringlets, more golden than sherry,
    Will fuddle as well the poor brain.

If wine makes us dupes, love is able
    To turn us to fools with like ease:
If the one lays us under the table,
    T'other brings us at least to our knees.

More tapering necks than the bottle's,
    With mouths more bewildering crowned,
Will pour from their ravishing throttles
    A stream that a sage would confound.

No spirit so ardent as woman's—
    So sure to intoxicate man;
Her touch is " delirium tremens"
    That maddens him more than the can.

Not the wines of fair Cyprus, the rover,
    So much as its women beguile—
Better rest where he is, " half-seas-over,"
    Than steer for so fatal an isle!

Oh, then, shun such a tempter as this is,
    Nor commerce so hazardous court!
Who embarks on the waves of her tresses
    Will grieve that he ventured from *port*.

ALL. Bravo! Bravo!

COUNT. Now, mine host, as wine is so certain a cure for all the ills of life, fill us another cup, and, to the brim! to the brim, I say! I need it all to-day, I assure you. My heart is heavy, and I must soon return to the wars! Come, come, good mine host, another song!

POP. Well, then I'll give you something in the good old-fashioned style.

Song.—POPINJAY.

When things go well, 'tis a merry, merry world,
  And all is blithe and jolly;
We can dance and we can sing, and be happy as a king,
  While we banish melancholy.
When things go ill, 'tis a sorry, sorry world,
  And all is dark, and dreary:
Then we mope, and then we scowl, and are sulky as an owl,
  While our life drags on a-weary,
But taking what we meet,
Both the bitter and the sweet,
  'Tis a very good world as we find it.

When woman smiles—Oh! she blossoms like the rose!
  And charms our hearts as sweetly;
She's a cure for every ill, and can turn us as she will,
  For she rules us all completely.
When woman frowns—she is quite another thing,
  So changed we stare and wonder;
Her glory withers all, while her sugar turns to gall,
  And her gentle words to thunder!
But taking what we meet,
Both the bitter and the sweet,
  She's a very good thing as we find her.

ALL. Bravo! bravo!

COUNT. That's a hearty good song! But pass the bottle! Give me wine for my consolation in all life's trials! Fortune may frown, friends desert us, and sweethearts denounce us, but the bottle alone, that faithful emblem of constancy, remains true to the last. Fill up, my friends, and before we part, let's sing the glories of the bottle!

Bacchanalian—The Bottle.—COUNT, *with Chorus.*

  Fill, my boys, for care's a sin:
    Bliss from drinking takes its growth;
  For grief flows out as wine flows in—
    There is not room for both.

CHORUS.

Then fill, boys, fill with a will!
  Whoever is sad, let him fill!
For deep and rare must be the care
  The bottle cannot kill.

Does your girl look cold or shy?
  In the glass a mistress view,
Whose rosy face and sparkling eye
  Are ever warm and true.
    Chorus. Then fill, &c.

When debts come in you cannot pay—
  Do not try the halter yet;
Dash down the liquid! that's the way
  To liquidate the debt.
    Chorus. Then fill, &c.

Have you lost a friend? alas!
  Droop not for we all must die;
But drop a tear within the glass,
  And drink his memory!
    Chorus. Then fill, &c.

All our joys may fade, and leave
  A void behind them. Let them fly!
No void, save one, can make us grieve—
  'Tis when the bottle's dry.
    Chorus. Then fill, &c.

[COUNT, POPINJAY, and JACQUES, *retire into the house. The others, after bidding good night, pass off, except* CLAUDE, *who remains sitting at the table quite melancholy.*

Enter GIPSY.

GIPSY.   Well, I have raised a pretty breeze!
    And yet I only sought to teaze,
    Not torture these enamored dears,
    Now set so sharply by the ears;

My heart no malice moves, but fun ;
And softens when my frolic's done.
And now my conscience pricks me sore
Some oil upon their wounds to pour ;
And first, the mischief to repair,
I'll soothe yon moping lover there.
[*To* CLAUDE.] How now ! sad youth, your revels prove
    Even boasted wine no cure for love,
    Obey me ! and success is clear—
    A golden maxim—persevere.
CLAUDE. [*Coming forward.*]
    But if she scorn and will not hear—
GIPSY. Persevere—persevere !
CLAUDE. Should she hold another dear—
GIPSY. Still I tell you, persevere !
CLAUDE. Should she jilt me, pretty seer ?
GIPSY. Never fear, persevere !
    To the end still persevere !
    Her window seek at moonlight hour,
    And in a song your sorrows pour !
    The moon keeps ward of maiden's heart,
    And opes it to the minstrel's art :
    Bait with the cheese that moons supply,
    You'll trap your maid however sly !
           [*Exit* CLAUDE.

Enter DAME P. *from the house.*

DAME P. Good Gipsy ! hold ! a word if you please—you
gipsies are so knowing. How shall I move my old man to
open his heart, and give me a new bonnet in time for the
coming fair ? I've worried him till I'm tired, and all
without effect, except to set him more and more against it.
GIPSY. There's naught man likes to pay for less
    Than what pertains to woman's dress :

As if in vengeance for the fall,
That brought the need to dress at all.
Your lord is not too prone to thrift,
But loathes this urging to a gift :
He knows your wish ; he's wise, and kind—
Say naught ! the gift will come, you'll find !

> [*Exit* DAME P. *into the house.*

ANNETTE *enters, and passes towards the house.*

What ! all unguarded—pretty queen !
Your lovers find you cold, I ween—
There's one I know.has burst your bars
To follow the less cruel wars.

ANN. No fear ! he will not really go—
GIPSY. He may, if you misuse him so.
Beware ! a youngster of our tribe
Went soldiering late—at glory's bribe ;
But soon returned—and all undone !
A leg, an arm, an eye were gone !—
But hark ! the cuckoo wakes the eve—
And homeward bound, I take my leave—
But with soft airs, and warblers' song,
My lonely path will not seem long.

Duet.—ANNETTE *and* GIPSY.

BOTH. O ! sweetly sighs the evening breeze,
That kisses all the blossomed trees ;
And sweetly, mid the boughs above,
The songsters pour their lay of love.
GIPSY. Warbles the cuckoo—
ANN. Answers the echo—
BOTH. And the soft murmuring floats through the grove.

BOTH. How peacefully the day declines !
How clear the rosy water shines !
While all the air—around—above—
Is vocal with the gush of love !

Gipsy.	Warbles the cuckoo—
Ann.	Answers the echo—
Both.	And the soft murmuring floats through the grove.

[Exeunt Annette *into the Cottage.*

SCENE II.—*The same by moonlight.*

Enter Claude *with a guitar.*

Claude. I'm not much in the humor for singing, but the Gipsy thinks it might soften Annette. Besides, it would hardly do to let her birthday go by without a serenade. I'll sing as softly as I can, for I would not like to wake the old man. I hope there are no dogs about.

Serenade.—Claude, *with guitar accompaniment.*

Sleep, gentle maiden, I would not wake thee,
  Only thy slumbering thought would I guide;
Dream that thy lover his passion is breathing,
  Drawn by the moonlight to mourn at thy side.

Hear me, yet wake not, scarce would my 'plaining
  Move you to doubt if you dream, or you hear;
Softly, as zephyr now sighs o'er your tresses,
  So would my murmuring creep to your ear.

Gentle lute, hush thee, lest thy fond wailing
  Heave the soft waves of her bosom too high;
Wafting dear wishes, to dreams will we leave her,
  Sweeter than tenderest vows we could sigh.

Jacques. [*Looking out at the door.*] Who's that, I wonder? Ah! I see—'tis Claude—come a sparking Annette. I'll titillate his torpidity.

[Jacques *goes out, then appears at the side, and imitates the bark of a dog.* Claude *hides himself.* Jacques *runs into the house.*

Pop. [*Appearing at the window with a blunderbuss.*] Who's making all that noise there at this time of night?

Who's there, I say? If I could only see the rascal once I'd pepper his jacket for him. Who are you? catterwauling about the streets at this hour. I wonder if that scapegrace, Jacques, is at his tricks again. Whoever you are, you'd better keep your breath to cool your porridge! disturbing quiet folks at midnight. . [*Grumbling.*

DAME P. [*Looking over his shoulders.*] Yes, and quiet folk's wives, too, to say nothing about landed proprietors!

POP. Out on you, wife, what are you doing here? To bed! to bed! I say. [*Shuts the window and exeunt.*

CLAUDE. [*Coming forward timidly.*] I'm sorry the old man was disturbed, for he's my friend—I had better steal off before I'm discovered.

[ANNETTE *appears at the lattice.*

Duet.—CLAUDE *and* ANNETTE.

ANN. Who with his minstrelsy wakes me to-night?
CLAUDE. Who but thy lover's self claims that sweet right?
ANN. Hist! for my father would rave should he hear—
CLAUDE. Love! while thou smilest, whose frowns can I fear?
BOTH. The gentle moon looks mildly down,
At her sweet gaze the vapors flee:
Ah! thus, when clouds around me frown,
Thy glance shall chase them, love, from me.
The night-bird's song
Calms nature's breast,
So thy dear voice
Soothes mine to rest.
Ever, when moonlight
Silvers the tree,
Music from slumber
Shall win me to thee. *Exeunt.*

END OF ACT II

ACT III.

SCENE—*The same, at Morning.*

Curtain rises on a Group of Peasants, listening to a distant hunt.

Duet.—POPINJAY *and* CLAUDE, *with chorus of men.*

Pop.	Hark! the hunters on the chase
CHORUS.	Hark! Hark!
CLAUDE.	Hark the hunters on the chase!
CHORUS.	Hark! Hark!
	Hark the hunters on the chase,
	The hounds in rapid race,
	The merry horns resounding loud!
	The bounding stag afar,
	Avoids the unequal war,
	As close his fleet pursuers crowd.
	The mountain rejoices
	With horns and with voices!
CLAUDE.	Sweetly the startled woodbirds sing,
	As dell and mountain merrily ring!
BASSES.	Hark! Hark!
TENORS.	Hark the horn! the merry horn!
	Hark! Hark!
BASSES.	Hark the hunters on the chase, &c.
	Tan-ta-ra-ra! Tan-ta-ra-ra!
ALL.	Hark! Hark! [*Exeunt all but* CLAUDE.

CLAUDE. What strange creatures these women are! Now, last night Annette was as kind to me as I could wish after having treated me during the day with neglect and contempt—to be repeated, perhaps, to-morrow. Well, let her use me as she will, I somehow cannot help hanging about her, in spite of myself.

Song.—CLAUDE.

Mischievous maiden! wayward and teasing—
  Now warm as summer, and now wintry cold—
Melting or freezing, paining or pleasing—
  How shall I seize thee? and how shall I hold?

No cloud of summer, leisurely floating,
  Changes so strangely, yet radiantly still.
Mischievous maiden! scorning or doting,
  Still must I follow thee, spite of my will.

Enter ANNETTE, *from the house.*

ANN. What is that you are mumbling there, Master Claude? Thank you for your thoughts!

CLAUDE. What should I be talking or thinking about but you? Oh, Annette! do not deny me any longer.

ANN. Deny you? deny you what? What is it you seek?

CLAUDE. You know it is your love I seek! Oh! when will you grant it?

ANN. Not so fast—not so fast, my good friend. Love leads to marriage, and marriage too often leads to indifference, humdrum, wrangling, and all sorts of terrible consequences. So important a matter demands reflection. As Jacques would say, "I will give the subject my most 'distinguished consideration.'"

Duet.—CLAUDE *and* ANNETTE.

CLAUDE.   Say! wilt thou yield, dear maid,
        And with thy sweetness feed my heart?

          Oh! why should rapture be delayed
          That must at best so soon depart?

ANN.   Not so fast, not so fast, gentle youth, if you please,
          You would bring me to care from a life full of ease;
          For this marriage, I'm told, has its thorns with its rose,
          And bride-cake, 'neath the crust, lacks the sugar it shows.
          Then your husband grows cross, as the novelty's gone,
          When a button comes off, or the meat's overdone.
          So crabbed and crusty, so savage and sour—
          That a girl should think well ere she gets in his power!

CLAUDE.   Say! wilt thou yield?

ANN.   We shall see!

CLAUDE.   Why so cruel, maiden dearest?
          Oh! what can it be that thou fearest?

ANN.   Why so hasty? do not press me!
          Oh! cease to annoy and distress me!

BOTH.   If 'tis true that the happiest life as is stated,
          Is when loving hearts blend together, well mated;
          And if sure that our own were by sympathy plighted,
          'Twere folly so coldly to keep disunited.

CLAUDE.   Ah! hear me now!

ANN.   Ah! spare me now—
          Some day I may listen.

CLAUDE.   No time like the present.

ANN.   Oh, cease with your prayers

CLAUDE.   No! they shall be incessant.
          Ah! then yield!

ANN.   Must I yield?

CLAUDE.   Dearest! say, wilt thou yield?

ANN. [*Pretending to hesitate.*] We shall see!

                 [ANNETTE *runs off,* CLAUDE *following.*

Enter GIPSY, *looking after them, smilingly.*

GIPSY.   No need to fan these rustic fires!
          The lady's case more care requires;
          My plot is laid—she joins the chase—
          But will her steed pursue the race?
          I've won the farrier of our tribe
          To prick his foot—a kiss the bribe.

He cannot farther speed than here—
The Count is nigh—the rest is clear.
A counsel in her ear I'll pour,
To test her truant love once more !   [*Exit.*

Enter LADY FLORA, MARIE, *and* PAUL.

MARIE. I'm rejoiced to meet you, my lady. You rode so
rapidly that we could scarce keep sight of you ; and here I
find you at last, at the village, and on foot. You did not
fall, my lady ?

FLORA. Oh no, Marie. Having joined the chase to draw
my mind from painful thoughts, I dashed along rather
recklessly, I suppose, when my horse fell lame, and I
thought it best to dismount, and wait for assistance. Paul,
look out yonder for some of the household, and order my
carriage !   [*Exit* PAUL

Enter GIPSY.

Proud lady, list ! but not with scorn,
The warning of the lowly born.
Beware ! thou stand'st upon a brink
Should cause thy inmost soul to shrink.
Retire ! whate'er thy pride it cost !
One forward step, and all is lost !
Thy soldier love is not untrue—
Thou dost him wrong ! haste to undo !
Once more confront him with the queen—
His truth, thy error, will be seen.
This warning heed, thy woes are healed ;
Despise it, and thy doom is sealed !   [*Exit.*

FLORA. What means this mockery ? [*To* PAUL, *who
enters.*] Paul, follow that girl quickly ! She is fleet of
foot, and will escape, without your utmost vigilance. Se-
cure her, and bring her to me ! [*Exit* PAUL.] [*Angrily.*]
We shall see if I am to be affronted with impunity by
every vagrant that chances to cross my path ! .

MARIE. Oh, my lady! do not despise the gipsy's warning. Whether by means of wit or witchcraft, she is shrewd and wise; and I know, says only the truth, in regard to this sad difference between yourself and the poor Count.

FLORA. [*Much excited.*] What, Marie! would you, too, presume to counsel me? 'Tis sufficiently mortifying to encounter the wild ravings of this vagabond Bohemian, without having to submit my conduct to the strictures of my own followers!

MARIE. Oh, pardon me, my dearest lady! I must speak, for my heart is overflowing. Am I not your foster-sister, your playmate, and the dearest friend of your childhood? and will you not, for the memory of those early days, bear with your poor Marie for one little offence?

FLORA. [*With feeling—seizing her hand.*] Marie, forgive me! From you I will bear anything—say on.

MARIE. Count Ernest still loves you—has always been faithful to you; and yet your impetuous feelings have so blinded your reason, so distorted appearances, and exposed your dearest interests to such great hazard, that unless some turn be taken—and promptly, too—they may be sacrificed beyond remedy. It is this necessity, my dear lady, which makes me bold to speak.

FLORA. Go on.

MARIE. I have spoken with Annette. She assures me the Count made her no show of affection beyond what gallantry required of him on the day of her fête.

FLORA. But the ring, Marie! that jeweled ring?

MARIE. 'Twas only a birthday present! costly, to be sure—but he had probably nothing else at hand to give. Besides, a gentleman must give handsomely if he give at all.

FLORA. Oh, Marie! my heart is not stone, and listens but too readily to these excuses which you urge in his behalf—but my judgment must be satisfied. How could he have been attracted by another, even for a moment, when he had almost reached me on his return, and when he must have known that I was so anxiously awaiting his coming ?

MARIE. He could not have known this. Your letters had miscarried—he had learned nothing of you for months together. Had he first seen you, and found you unchanged —oh, believe me, my lady, he could not then have turned to any other.

FLORA. What you say has certainly some show of reason, but—

MARIE. O, do not hesitate, my good lady ! you may drive him to desperation. Sunk in despondency by your coldness, he first sought to rouse himself by wine, and has since determined to return at once to the wars. O ! my lady ! you have a just, as well as kindly heart—to that I appeal. The Gipsy has suggested, most wisely, that the Count be put to the test, by confronting him again with Annette—this, you must surely grant, is but an act of simple justice to him, and this is all I ask. Should he fail under the trial, your faithful Marie will be the last to stay his final condemnation.

FLORA. [*Softened.*] Oh ! Marie ! I own the infirmity of a hasty nature, and feel but too deeply how easily it might have hurried me into error ; although the evidence seemed insurmountable. On reflection, it does appear but reasonable to allow the Count an opportunity to exonerate himself—so to that issue will I refer the final disposition of this painful question. You may therefore call Annette, and admit her to our confidence. Explain to her my difficulty with the Count, because of his marked attentions to her yesterday—which, you believe he would not have shown had he first seen me, and been assured of my constancy. Say also that we have decided to put the gentleman to the proof, by engaging her now to throw herself in his way, with a view to entice him to another *tête-a-tête* in the grove. See this fairly done, my good Marie! and I promise you, if the Count stand firm under the temptation, I shall believe that I have condemned him unjustly: and will be found, I trust, as ready to make reparation for an error, as I was hasty in the commission of it.

MARIE. Oh! my dear lady! I am only too happy to obey you. [*Exit.*

FLORA. Oh! maiden pride! forgive me if I stoop too far in this last effort to recover my lost love. It is perhaps but a slender chance—and yet hope, and a lingering tenderness—must I own it?—urge me on.

Enter MARIE *with* ANNETTE.

FLORA. My good Annette! you have the power to serve me in a matter of some moment—as Marie has, doubtless, informed you—and I cannot question your readiness to oblige me on this, as well as on all other occasions.

ANN. You may use me as you will in this matter, my lady! and I will serve you faithfully. [*Aside.*] To say truth, I rather like the sport.

FLORA. But you must tempt the gentleman strongly— you must spread all your toils—all your fascinations—you little coquette.

ANN. Depend upon me! my lady! I'll not spare him.

FLORA. Hush! here he comes! Poor fellow! how sad he looks!

MARIE. Now, let us step aside and observe him, while Annette puts him to the test.

FLORA. Let me retire, Marie! while you remain to witness the trial, and bring me tidings of the result.

MARIE. Nay, my good lady—your own eyes observed his seeming inconstancy, and it is but just that they should now be witness to what, I feel sure, will prove to be his triumph and justification. [*Exeunt.*

Enter COUNT ERNEST.

COUNT. Was ever woman so unreasonable as Flora! To drive me from her with such hasty violence, and for what offence I am utterly at a loss to imagine. Impetuous as she is, at the slightest wound to her feelings, in her cooler moments I have always found her incapable of injustice, and overflowing with tenderness : and yet, unless some kindly accident should unravel the present entanglement, such is her pride that I know she would sacrifice all —even her affection—sooner than bend her nature to the slightest advance towards a reconciliation. Why then do I linger here? I cannot tear myself from her neighborhood —I cannot drive her from my thoughts. I must seek her once more before parting with her forever—even at the hazard of another, and a sterner repulse. Her indignation might be endured, but her absence is insupportable.

Song.—COUNT.

Absent from thee! what deeper woe
   Than absence, gloomy solitude?
I better bore thine anger's glow
   Than the dull peace which has ensued.
Give but mine eyes thy form again!
   Give but mine ears thy quickening voice!
And though thy glances flash disdain,
   And words speak daggers, I'll rejoice!

Absent from thee! O! I'd forgive
   Whate'er reproach thou mad'st me bear,
And even thy fury's rage outlive,
   To know but this, that thou wert near.
I must return—though doubly curst—
   Though all thy lightnings scathe my brain—
I heed them not—I've known the worst—
   For absence owns no master pain,

Enter ANNETTE *singing*—*" O such is the lover,"* &c.

Count. [*Aside*.]. So, here comes my little Queen again !
[Annette *beckons*.] This village coquette would lure me
on to another rural *tête-a-tête*. But I am in no mood for
trifling now. I have no heart for gallantry to-day.

QUARTET and CHORUS.

Ann.	To the woodland, come !
Count.	No, no I've no heart for sport to-day,
	Pretty tempter, hence, away !
Ann.	A gallant, gallant soldier, you !
	To leave a pretty maid to sue.
Both.	The fields are gay as yesterday,
	The warblers sing as sweetly,
	Yet comes a change so dark and strange
	It saddens you (me) completely.
Ann.	You love another, and fain would win her ?
Count	Most true !
Ann.	Well ! if you truly love her,
	I'll try if I can move her
	To spare her suffering lover.

[MARIE leads forward FLORA.

There—take her.

[The COUNT and FLORA embrace.

FLORA *and* ANNETTE.	Joy ! for the strife is over, Now proved the faithful lover, The bitter pain of trials past Gives sweeter bliss at last.
Count.	I'm with amazement dumb ! Oh ! rapture new ! Can this be true ?
[*To* ANNETTE.]	Ah ! coquette you have betrayed me ! 'Tis a sorry trick you've played me !
Count *and* Flora.	Now while every blessing Thus at last possessing, Linked in peace together, By Love's silken tether, Nevermore to sever, We'll love, and love forever !
Claude.	Dear Annette, their rapture see ! They are blest, and why not we ?

FLORA.	Come ! no longer cruel be,
	There's no truer lad than he.
ANN.	Well ! I had hoped to shun the snare,
	But if I must—I must—beware !

{ *Peasants enter behind.* } But if I must—I must—so there !   [*Coquettishly.*

[*Gives her hand to* CLAUDE—*they embrace.*

Chorus. Joy ! for the strife is over ! &c.

POP. [*Coming forward.*] Well upon my word ! this is beautiful— Mrs. P. You shall have the bonnet ! Embrace me ! Every body is getting reconciled to every body. Every body is smiling upon every body, and every body is going to marry every body, and, like the end of a fairy tale, I suppose every body is going to live in peace, and——

JACQUES. And die in a jar of oleaginous culinary compound.

POP. Ah ! here is young hopeful again ! I thought we had been very quiet for some time.

Enter PAUL, *dragging in* GIPSY.

PAUL. Here she is at last, my lady ! but she tried my wind for me, I can tell you. Whew ! why she runs like a deer.

FLORA. Young woman, it is well for you that you meet me at a time when the general joy has so softened my resentment, that I have not the heart to condemn you to any but the lightest punishment. I shall therefore only require that you and your tribe withdraw at once from a neighborhood where your presence excites in this good family so many painful reminiscenes. Do this and you are forgiven.

GIPSY. Lady ! the doom you deem so light
More awes than threat of dungeon night.
There's something in these groves and streams
That minds me of my early dreams :
A glory lingers on this sky
Trailed from the morn of infancy:

Here could I ever love to rest—
Oh Lady ! waive thy stern behest !
With chains or stripes I were content ;
But doom me not to banishment !
    [LADY FLORA *waves her hand refusing her.*
Well, as thou wilt, I must obey: [*Submissively.*
But grant one kindly grace, I pray,
To sweeten thy severe command—
O, let me dare to kiss that hand !

[FLORA *offers her hand to* GIPSY, *who kneels to kiss it, when* DAME P. *discovers a golden heart hanging from her neck.*

DAME P. How came you by that trinket ? That was lost with my child !   It was given to her by the good Baron at her baptism.   Tell me the truth, girl !   Where did you get this ?

GIPSY.   I know not—since my earliest day
      That charm upon my bosom lay.

DAME P. This girl must surely belong to the tribe that stole my child !

FLORA. Hold ! a suspicion breaks upon me ! may it not be the lost child herself who now stands before us ?
                    [*Emotion in the crowd.*

Dame P. Here ! stand aside all—I can settle that question—I would know her among a thousand ! one mark is sufficient—her brother once carelessly shot an arrow high into the air, which fell and wounded the child between the shoulders, leaving a scar too singular to be ever mistaken. Make way there ! and let me look at her ! [*She examines the* GIPSY *and finds the scar.*] Good angels ! save us—there is the very mark ! I would swear to it anywhere.   My child ! my child ! [*Embracing her. To* POPINJAY.] Peter! it is our own dear child ! our lost daughter Alice !

Pop. Merciful heaven! it must indeed be so! [*Embracing her.*

Trio and Sestet.

FLORA, COUNT, GIPSY, ANNETTE, CLAUDE, POPINJAY.

Oh, day of wonder! Oh, day of joy!
Golden with rapture, without alloy:
Even its tempests, startling with dread,
Burst into blessings showered on our head!
Joined are the parted—lost ones are found:
All hearts that sorrowed now lightly bound.
Oh, day of wonder! &c.

DAME P. Yes! yes! there can be no mistake! I might have known her by her bright eyes, and sweet smile. Poor child! how much she must have suffered!

[ALICE *shakes hands with those about her, and embraces* JACQUES.

JACQUES. [*Aside*] "I shot this sparrow,
            With my bow and arrow!"

Pop. [*Much moved.*] Oh! that I should live to see her once more alive! what a lucky, lucky day! tol-lol-de-rol! —I'm so happy!   [*Laughing and sobbing.*

JACQUES. Happy—why, dad! what makes you so lachrymose, if you're so jubilant?

Pop. I tell you I am happy—the happiest dog alive! tol-de-rol! [*Dancing about and embracing all around him.*] I feel as if I could love everybody to-day.

DAME P. Hoity-toity! Mr P.—do keep your joy within decent bounds!

Pop. What! would you put a curb to our happiness at such a time as this? Is not this a day to be forever remembered? Have not the Count and the lady after great trials and tribulations become reconciled? Have not Claude and Annette at length agreed to buckle to? Have not you and I settled our difficulties about the bonnet question? Has not the good Baron given us the Briar Cottage? and last, but most astonishing of all, is not the lost lamb restored to her fold? Have all these wonders taken place in a day, and shall we not rejoice? Aye—that we will, and right heartily too, I can promise you—wine there—good wife—and plenty of it too, and of the best. Let everybody drink to the happiness of everybody !

[All fill.

FINALE *and* CHORUS.

POP.   Friends and neighbors! Pass the bottle! all be joyful!
     Come! a merry—merry toast!
CHORUS OF MEN.   Fill! Fill!
CLAUDE.   Here's to the maid that of love is not afraid!
     And keeps true through the ills that assail us—
COUNT. And here's to the wife! that's the comfort of our life!
     When pain and misfortune quail us—
CHORUS.And here's to the bowl! the solace of the soul,
     When the wives, and the sweethearts fail us.

ANN.   And here's to the man that keeps constant—if he can—
     Till our smiles make amends for our scorning!
FLORA. Here's to the knight that would battle for the right!
     Every post of the soldier adorning:
ALL. And here's happiness to all! who will pleasantly recall
     Our merry Gipsy's day of frolic, and of warning—
       Again! Here's happiness to all
        Around us !

THE END.

INDEX

OF

SONGS AND CONCERTED PIECES.